Ladybird Readers

Rex the Big Dinosaur

Series Editor: Sorrel Pitts
Text adapted by Sorrel Pitts
Illustrated by Kim Geyer

LADYBIRD BOOKS

UK | USA | Canada | Ireland | Australia
India | New Zealand | South Africa

Ladybird Books is part of the Penguin Random House group of companies
whose addresses can be found at global.penguinrandomhouse.com.
www.penguin.co.uk   www.puffin.co.uk   www.ladybird.co.uk

Penguin
Random House
UK

First published 2017
001

Copyright © Ladybird Books Ltd, 2017

Printed in China

A CIP catalogue record for this book is available from the British Library

ISBN: 978-0-241-29741-4

All correspondence to
Ladybird Books
Penguin Random House Children's
80 Strand, London WC2R 0RL

Rex the Big Dinosaur

Picture words

red dinosaurs

small dinosaurs

4

5

Rex is a big dinosaur. He sees some small dinosaurs. They are playing.

"Can I play, too?" asks Rex.

"Yes," say the small dinosaurs. "You can play with us."

Rex runs behind the small dinosaurs. He shows his big teeth.

The small dinosaurs do not like Rex's big teeth. They run from him!

Rex sees the small dinosaurs again. They are playing.

"Can I play, too?" asks Rex.

"Yes," say the small dinosaurs. "You can play with us."

Rex opens his mouth and roars. It is a very big roar!

The small dinosaurs hear Rex roar. They run from him.

Rex sees the small
dinosaurs again.

"Can I play with you?"
he asks them.

"No," say the small dinosaurs. "You are too big. You have got big teeth, and your roar is very big. We don't like it!"

"Please go," say
the small dinosaurs.

Rex goes. He is sad.

19

Then, Rex sees some red dinosaurs. These red dinosaurs can fly. The small dinosaurs do not like the red dinosaurs.

Rex runs behind the red dinosaurs. He roars, and shows his big teeth.

The red dinosaurs do not like Rex's big teeth. They fly from Rex and the small dinosaurs.

The small dinosaurs
are happy.

"Play with us again,
Rex!" they say.

Rex does not roar.

The small dinosaurs are happy, and Rex is happy, too.

27

Activities

The key below describes the skills practiced in each activity.

 Spelling and writing

 Reading

 Speaking

 Critical thinking

Preparation for the Cambridge Young Learners Exams

1 Look and read. Put a ✓ or a ✗ in the boxes. 📖 ⬤

1

This is Rex.   ✓

2

These are big dinosaurs.   ☐

3

These are red dinosaurs.   ☐

4

These are teeth.   ☐

5

ROAR

Rex has got a small roar.   ☐

2 **Look and read. Write *yes* or *no*.**

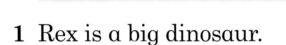

Rex is a big dinosaur. He sees some small dinosaurs. They are playing.

"Can I play, too?" asks Rex.

"Yes," say the small dinosaurs. "You can play with us."

1 Rex is a big dinosaur.   yes

2 The small dinosaurs
are playing.   ....

3 There are six
small dinosaurs.   ....

4 Rex wants to play, too.   ....

5 The small dinosaurs
say, "No. You cannot
play with us."   ....

3 **Look at the letters.**
Write the words.

1 r d e

   r e d

2 s l l m a

3 x e R

4 t e t e h

5 r r a o

4 **Circle the correct sentences.** 📖

1
   a Rex runs behind
     the small dinosaurs.
   b The small dinosaurs
     run behind Rex.

2
   a Rex shows his
     small teeth.
   b Rex shows his
     big teeth.

3
   a The small dinosaurs
     do not like Rex's teeth.
   b The small dinosaurs
     like Rex's big teeth.

4
   a Rex runs from the
     small dinosaurs.
   b The small dinosaurs
     run from Rex.

5 **Find the words.** 📖

(b	i	g)	b	e	c	w	f	t
a	d	s	m	a	l	l	e	e
q	y	i	r	e	p	h	y	e
d	i	n	o	s	a	u	r	t
e	z	j	a	o	k	s	y	h
m	a	x	r	t	p	l	a	y
g	i	b	q	b	p	t	v	o
a	o	w	s	d	q	a	f	m

big

dinosaur

small

play

roar

teeth

6 **Talk about the pictures with a friend. How are they different? Use the words in the box to help you.** 🗩

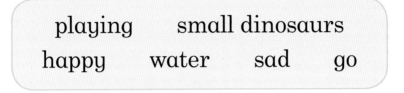

playing   small dinosaurs
happy   water   sad   go

a

b

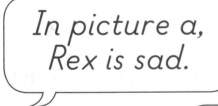

In picture a,
Rex is sad.

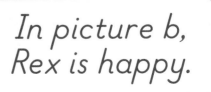

In picture b,
Rex is happy.

7 **Circle the correct words.**

Rex sees the small dinosaurs again. They are playing.

"Can I play, too?" asks Rex.

"Yes," say the small dinosaurs. "You can play with us."

1 Rex sees the (**small**)/ **big** dinosaurs again.

2 The small dinosaurs are **running.** / **playing.**

3 "Can **I** / **you** play, too?" asks Rex.

4 **"Yes,"** / **"No,"** say the small dinosaurs.

5 "You can play with **them.**" / **us.**"

8 Write *play* or *playing*.

1 The small dinosaurs are
   playing.

2 "Can I ...., too?" asks Rex.

3 "You can .... with us,"
   say the small dinosaurs.

4 "Can I .... with you?"
   asks Rex.

5 The small dinosaurs like ....
   with Rex now.

9 **Look and read. Choose the correct words and write them on the lines.** 📖 ✏️ ✳️

Rex opens his mouth and roars. It is a very big roar!

The small dinosaurs hear Rex roar. They run from him.

ROAR

---

hear   opens   run   big

---

1 Rex _opens_ his mouth and roars.

2 It is a very .... roar!

3 The small dinosaurs .... Rex roar.

4 They .... from him.

10 **Circle the correct pictures.** 📖 ❓

1 Rex wants to play with them.

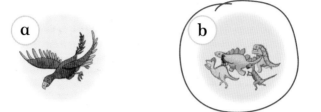

2 The small dinosaurs are not happy.

3 This dinosaur is nice.

4 This dinosaur can fly.

11 Do the crossword. 📖 ✏️

Down

1 These dinosaurs can fly.

3 Rex is . . . at the end of the story.

Across

2 Rex opens his mouth, and shows these.

4 Rex is a . . . dinosaur.

5 The small dinosaurs hear Rex . . .

12 **Match the two parts of the sentences.** 📖

1 Rex

2 Rex cannot

3 The red dinosaurs

4 "Can I play, too?"

5 The small dinosaurs

a play with the small dinosaurs.

b asks Rex.

c shows his big teeth.

d run from Rex.

e fly from Rex.

13 Read the text. Choose the correct words and write them next to 1—5.

dinosaurs   fly   goes   red   sad

"Please go," say the small

¹ _dinosaurs_ . Rex ² _____.

He is ³ _____. Then, Rex

sees some ⁴ _____ dinosaurs.

These dinosaurs can ⁵ _____.

14 **Write *He* or *They*.** 📖 ✏️

1 Rex runs. ___He___ is behind the red dinosaurs.

2 Rex roars. _____ shows his big teeth.

3 The red dinosaurs see Rex's teeth. _____ do not like his big teeth.

4 _____ fly from Rex.

5 _____ fly from the small dinosaurs, too.

15 **Ask and answer questions about Rex and the red dinosaurs with a friend.** 🗨

> Rex runs behind the red dinosaurs. He roars, and shows his big teeth.
>
> The red dinosaurs do not like Rex's big teeth. They fly from Rex and the small dinosaurs.

ROAR

1 *Who does Rex run behind?*

He runs behind the red dinosaurs.

2 What does Rex show?

3 Do the red dinosaurs like Rex?

4 What do the red dinosaurs do?

16 Look at the pictures. Look at the letters. Put a ✓ by the correct words.

1

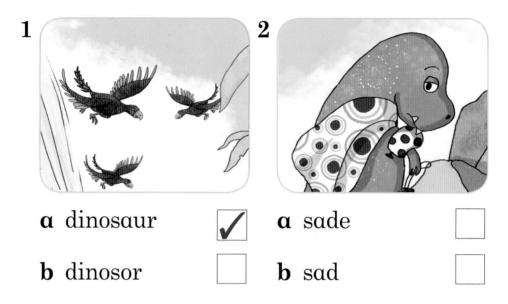

a dinosaur ✓

b dinosor ☐

2

a sade ☐

b sad ☐

3

a teef ☐

b teeth ☐

4

a play ☐

b pley ☐

17 Write the missing letters.

1 Rex sees some red
dinos a u rs.

2 They can fl_____.

3 The small dinosaurs
are happ_____.

4 "Pl_____ _____ with us again,
Rex," they say.

5 "Play with us again, Rex,"
they s_____ _____.

18 **Read the questions. Write the answers.** 📖 ✏️

1 Are the red dinosaurs Rex's new friends?

No, they are not.

2 Do the red dinosaurs like Rex's big teeth?

No, _____.

3 Are the small dinosaurs and Rex friends now?

Yes, _____.

19 **Order the story. Write 1—5.**

.... These dinosaurs can fly.

......1...... Rex sees some red dinosaurs.

.... Rex is happy.

.... Rex roars, and the red dinosaurs fly from him.

.... The small dinosaurs are happy. They are Rex's friends.

Level 1

Anansi Helps
a Friend
978-0-241-25409-7 ☐

Cinderella
978-0-241-25407-3 ☐

The Enormous
Turnip
978-0-241-25408-0 ☐

On the Farm
978-0-241-25413-4 ☐

Cars
978-0-241-28354-7 ☐

Jon's Football
Team
978-0-241-25411-0 ☐

The Magic
Porridge Pot
978-0-241-25406-6 ☐

In the Garden
978-0-241-26220-7 ☐

Fun with
Old Things
978-0-241-26219-1 ☐

Fairy Friends
978-0-241-28351-6 ☐

Peter Rabbit
Goes to the Island
978-0-241-25415-8 ☐

Topsy and Tim
Go to the Zoo
978-0-241-25414-1 ☐

Topsy and Tim
Go to the Farm
978-0-241-28355-4 ☐

The Fair
978-0-241-28357-8 ☐

Daddy Pig's
Old Chair
978-0-241-28356-1 ☐

Rex the Big
Dinosaur
978-0-241-29741-4 ☐

Peter Rabbit and
the Radish Robber
978-0-241-29742-1 ☐

Topsy and Tim
Go to London
978-0-241-29743-8 ☐

On a Boat
978-0-241-29744-5 ☐

Baby Animals
978-0-241-29745-2 ☐

Now you're ready for Level 2!